The LANGUAGE OF DOVES

Rosemary Wells ✧ Pictures by Greg Shed

Dial Books for Young Readers ✦ New York

For Kay Cherry —R.W.

For David, Angelina, Josie, Luigi, Roberto, and Joe —G.S.

Published by Dial Books for Young Readers
A Division of Penguin Books USA Inc.
375 Hudson Street
New York, New York 10014

Text copyright © 1996 by Rosemary Wells
Pictures copyright © 1996 by Greg Shed
Design by Nancy R. Leo
Printed in Hong Kong
First Edition
1 3 5 7 9 10 8 6 4 2

Library of Congress Cataloging in Publication Data
Wells, Rosemary.
The language of doves / by Rosemary Wells; pictures by Greg Shed.—1st ed.
p.   cm.
Summary: On her sixth birthday Julietta's grandfather gives her one of his
beautiful homing pigeons and tells her a story of his experience raising and
training doves in Italy during the Great War.
ISBN 0-8037-1471-8 (trade).—ISBN 0-8037-1472-6 (lib. bdg.)
[1. Grandfathers—Fiction. 2. Homing pigeons—Fiction. 3. Pigeons—Fiction.
4. World War I, 1914-1918—Italy—Fiction. 5. Death—Fiction.]
I. Shed, Greg, ill. II Title.
PZ7.W46843Lan 1996   [E]—dc20   95-40283   CIP   AC

*The artwork was prepared using gouache on canvas. It was color-separated
and reproduced as red, blue, yellow, and black halftones.*

Author's Note

For thousands of years people have used homing pigeons
(or doves) to send messages through the air. The First World War
in particular abounds with stories of pigeon heroism. Nearly
invisible to enemy soldiers, the birds were faithful carriers of tiny
coded messages which alerted troops to any number of emergencies
or secrets. Feathered heroes and heroines saved the lives of soldiers
and sailors on both sides. The birds were given Medals of Honor and
all the highest military decorations a country could bestow. They are
remembered to this day by the armed services of the many nations
whose young men fought in this terrible war.

I can see us now, Grandfather and I, sitting on his Brooklyn rooftop. It is my sixth birthday. We are waiting for his doves to come home from Cape May, New Jersey. They were taken there by truck this morning with other flocks of racing pigeons. My grandfather watches the sky. "I have always spoken the language of doves, Julietta," he likes to say.

Grandfather names the doves for the great operas: Marcellina, Ottavio, Elvira, Alfredo. Before I could speak, I knew those names.

Today Grandfather has given me a birthday dove, too young to fly with the others. She is rosy gray, layered with cocoa brown. It is a feather color known as "Isabella," he tells me. "That is what I will call her," I say.

Grandfather frowns at the edge of the Brooklyn sky where he says it links up with the New Jersey sky. "I will tell you about another Isabella," he tells me, "in Italy, long ago and far away."

So on my sixth birthday I hear this story for the first time.

I had no mother or father. I was raised in a monastery by the Franciscan Brothers, with other orphan boys. I did not like to fight, so I stayed by myself in the roof garden. This garden had olive and fig trees and a statue of Saint Francis hundreds of years old. There was a dovecote there, under the red tile eaves where it was open to the mountain breeze.

When I was six like you, I learned to care for the birds. I began to speak their language. When I was seven, I was put in charge of the flock. There were eighty birds. I knew them all by name, but my favorite was a female the color of rain clouds. Of course I named her Isabella. The Brothers called her "Madrina," which means godmother. She was exactly that to me, only little.

In summer the Brothers sent me into the mountain forest to collect mushrooms. Growing along deer paths under certain trees were the most delicate parasols and morelli. Isabella, always on my shoulder, waited for me to write tiny messages telling the cook what I had found. I wrapped the papers around her leg and sent her flying back so the cook would know what to prepare for dinner.

I thought this quiet life would last forever, but one day the Great War began. Soon after, the army came to the monastery. They took the biggest boys and all the doves.

Without my Isabella I went into a spell of grieving and did not eat for seven days. But luckily for me two soldiers returned. They asked for the boy in charge of the doves, since the sergeant could do nothing with them. This was how, at nine years old, I was drafted into the army.

No one could tell me why the Italians were fighting the Austrians in the Alps. I didn't care because I was well away from any fighting, and my doves and I were warm with plenty to eat.

One day two lieutenants stopped at my captain's tent. They wanted three doves to take into battle. They chose two of my strongest males, Bruno and Alberto. Then they picked Isabella. I pleaded and cried and told them she was untrained, that she had a bad heart. But they said her color would be invisible to the enemy soldiers, so they took her.

I did not know what happened up there in the mountains until much later, when the soldiers who came back told me what they saw.

The first three days of battle two hundred soldiers were lost. When this happened, a message was put on Bruno's leg asking for help, telling where our army was hiding. But Bruno was shot down by the Austrians and his message intercepted.

In the next week many more soldiers were lost. When this happened, Alberto was sent with another message asking for help. But the Austrians had hawks trained to seek out pigeons. Alberto must have been snapped up in midair, because he and his message were never found.

When there were only a dozen men left, Isabella was lofted into the air. An Austrian marksman shot her as she rested in a pine tree. She fell to the ground, stunned and bleeding. The marksman fired again.

I did not know any of this at the time. I was waiting in camp, thinking only of my three gentle friends. In the place my heart usually beat was a hollow where the cold wind howled. Through the night I strained to hear the soft flutter of Isabella's wings. In my nine years in the world I had known only the love of this small cloud-colored bird.

Twelve days passed like twelve months. Isabella did not come. I thought I would grow to be a man who gazed upward at the skies my whole lifetime in case one day she would find me.

Then just at sunset I spotted what I thought was a rat crossing the mud near my tent. But it was not a rat. It was Isabella walking toward me, wings dragging uselessly. She was nearly dead.

The message giving our soldiers' location was still attached to her leg. Because of her bravery, eight men lived.

I cleaned her and fed her and repaired her hurt wings. Then I kept her deep inside my tunic so that she would heal and no one would ever take her again.

"Isabella sat comfortably on my shoulders for the rest of her years," Grand-father tells me. "But you know, she is a famous dove. At the end of the war the Italian High Command awarded her a silver medal on a purple ribbon."

Grandfather pulls out his wallet and shows me an old photograph so light and brown, I can hardly find the little bird. But she is there, on the shoulder of a thin smiling boy.

My Isabella comes home with me on the subway to Forest Hills in Queens. I carry her in a small box with chicken-wire windows.

Every Monday morning just before school I let Isabella fly. I hope she will return to me, but instead she sails quickly over to Grandfather's loft in Brooklyn. There is no getting her back until my Sunday visit with Grandfather.

"How does she know the way?" I ask Grandfather.

"Some people say doves memorize church steeples," he tells me. "Other people say that the magnetic forces in the earth guide them. But I know it is because they can smell smells only birds can detect."

After a year I give up training Isabella to come home to me. In her heart she is a Brooklyn girl, so when I release her Monday mornings it is always with a tiny "I love you" for Grandfather in an aluminum capsule attached to her leg.

The Sunday before I turn nine, Grandfather and I have a rooftop birthday party.

"Do you think Isabella will ever fly home to me, Grandfather?" I ask.

"Oh, yes," he answers. "When you've learned the language of doves."

A week after my birthday our telephone rings at dawn. I hear my mother and father cry and I know my grandfather has died.

I stay home from school. I think only of Isabella and our Sundays with Grandfather, which have vanished like the sun over the edge of the earth.

There is a long service in a Brooklyn church and then a long lunch in Grandfather's home. I cannot listen to people talking or the rustling of fancy clothes. I can't eat a morsel of the hundred dishes my aunts have brought in that day, nor do I want to say hello to the priest. I wander to the rooftop and find the dovecote empty.

Clattering down the stairs I cry to my uncle in a panic, "Where are the doves? Where is my Isabella?"

"Sold to a pigeon breeder in Providence, Rhode Island," comes the answer.

I cannot sleep that night. My mother tries to soothe me with a story. My father brings me a glass of warm milk. But even they go to bed at last, leaving me to gaze into the northern sky. I remember my grandfather's words: "In the place my heart usually beat was a hollow where the cold wind howled."

I fall asleep at five, but at six there is a scratching at my window. It is Isabella. She has come back to me for the first time. Probably she tried Grandfather's Brooklyn loft first and found it empty. She is tired from her long flight. I settle her on my pillow.

Around her leg is my aluminum message capsule. Grandfather missed my last "I love you," I think as I undo the capsule and unroll the scrap of paper.

But it is not my writing at all. It is a message to me in Grandfather's spidery old-country hand:

"Do not listen to a word they tell you. Having learned the language of doves I have learned also to fly. Watch for me."

And of course, Isabella and I always do.